# PIZZAZZ

## A PLAN FOR AGING

### WITH

### WITH GRACE AND STYLE

### BY

## KATE CEFOLIA MILLER

# DEDICATION

## TO THE MEN AND WOMEN IN MY FAMILY

*Who were examples of*

### *Aging With Pizzazz*

ESPECIALLY

## MY MOTHER

## PAULINE DUPUY CEFOLIA

## Who at 87

Continues to work at living fully

### *each moment.*

# ACKNOWLEDGMENTS

I would like to express my gratitude to all who helped make this possible, especially, Dorothy O'Brien who gave me valuable information and assistance with editing, as well as encouraging me to continue in this work.

My family who provide me love and support always
For each of you I am forever grateful.

Finally for my friends and co-workers
who make me feel that I can do anything.
Thank you.

# CONTENTS

# PROLOGUE

I have thought about writing this book for a long time. I see this book as a tool to jump-start those of us who are moving into our own aging. We must begin thinking about what it means to grow old in society today, to consider our options for continuing a fulfilling and meaningful life even into old age, to stay

# empowered,

and in charge of the direction our lives take throughout our aging. My wish is that this book is just a beginning work, challenging us to think, plan, and influence society in how they treat their old.

I am a social worker in the field of home health, and my primary client base is working with the aged population. Over the past twenty plus years I discovered that many people move into aging without considering how they will navigate this part of their life. Oh they often plan for some kind of financial stability for their 'retirement' years, but beyond that they sort of float into aging without much thought or planning for other aspects of aging that will affect most of us if we live long enough. Most of my work over these years has been to

# empower

elderly patients and their families to take charge of where they want to live, how they will take care of themselves, and how they will manage failing health, and increasing needs for assistance. I have worked also to empower families who are responsible for the care of older family members, so they can meet their own needs as well as the needs of the person they are trying to care for.

In the past, whenever I needed direction in a phase or challenge in my life, I have gone to someone else's experience to provide me with information as a jumping off point for my own decisions. I have done this often through reading books. Books have helped me blunder through adolescence, delighted me in childhood and provided me with a spiritual foundation as a young woman. Books have also provided direction for my life course. I became open to visions and dreams of multiple options before me.

I discovered that I had  choices

I can decide how I want to direct my life.  I learned that I was not a victim of circumstances, genetics, or my past.  My past is completed and filled with lessons learned, but

## the future is mine to create each day.

As I continue this journey, I find myself marching rather rapidly toward my sixties.   I have worked in the field of aging for most of my adult life. I worked as a nurse for ten years and have been doing social work for the past twenty-five years in the field of aging. I know a lot of facts about how we age emotionally as well as physically. I have walked the road through aging vicariously by watching others as their bodies or minds let them down. Often the people I worked with and even those in my own family found themselves forced into choices that were made by others. **They did not think about their own aging and consider decisions they could make in order to enhance the quality of their life and cope with the unexpected changes that aging brings along with it.**

There is a considerable amount of research in the field of aging. Often younger academics and health care professionals instruct even younger health care professionals on how to deal with us, in the complexities and challenges that come with the aging of our bodies. When I began to look for something to inspire me and give me a sense of optimism about my future, I realized that there is very little written about how to move through this part of our lives with a sense of hope and grace. There are some writings, but in my judgment they are in short supply.

There is some indication that health care professionals are beginning to recognize that there are developmental milestones and stages that we go through as we age. These developmental stages are much the same as we go through as an infant.  The difference is that

## we go in reverse!

Carol Flaherty, Montana State University Communications Services, Bozeman, Montana states that *"Although the 'declines' of aging are different and unpredictable, most people do experience them and have to make adjustments as their systems begin to behave less efficiently."*
An infant progresses through the growth stages that take him or her through the wondrous

milestones that lead to independence.

# THEY MARCH TOWARD ADULTHOOD

and the ability to manage their life in a purposeful manner in order to

### reach their goals          REALIZE THEIR DREAMS

and

## make their contribution to society.

Then they progress to creating and raising a family, and pursuing their life work whatever that may be.

As children we all anticipated becoming that

## MAGICAL ADULT

and having the power and freedom to make our mark on this world.

## Somewhere between eighteen and death we are considered old.

We are still adults when we are old, but often society and our American culture no longer consider us competent. An old person, who is competent and capable, is considered an exception, not the norm. We have all heard of individuals who have achieved great things as they aged. The image, however, that most of us carry in our mind is a person who is no longer able to make good decisions. The old are often considered cranky and selfish, someone who is using up many of our financial resources, and who drains the energy of their families expecting to be cared for in their own home until they die. The old are considered prime targets for crime due to loss of mental sharpness, which occurs, in advanced age, and diminishing physical strength.

*My personal belief is that maybe for the first time in history we have more choices about how we age then ever before.*

As baby-boomers

# TUMBLE

into aging our political and social systems are trying to figure out how to manage us. We have had opportunities for mental health growth and spiritual growth that many of our ancestors did not have.

We have access to large amounts of information through computers. We can travel more easily with air travel. The breakthroughs in medicine can keep us healthy for much longer than most of our ancestors ever thought.

I believe

## we can be an asset to society as we age

We can alter the prejudice that surrounds aging in this country,

### and we can truly live until we die.

I believe we can do this with knowledge, acceptance, and courage. I also believe this generation is up to the challenge

# THE CHOICE IS UP TO US

# CHAPTER ONE

## CHALLENGES

*"What she mostly wanted, he learned,*
*was the same thing many people want---*
*someone to notice she was there."*
*Mitch Albom Tuesday's with Morrie*
*Page 110*

We are still adults when we get old, but things they are a changing. When I was approaching fifty all of my preconceived images of aging began to haunt me. I remember when I was in my twenties and new in nursing, if someone in their late forties or fifties died I thought that "well they have had a long life it isn't too sad." As I approached my fifties, my insides were fighting and screaming out, no I'm not old, there is still a whole lot of life left inside of me. The first assault to bring the reality to me that I was no longer 'young' was an invitation to join AARP. I immediately threw everything away. No way, was I going to have anything like "Modern Maturity" coming into my home, I was too young.

The year before I turned fifty, I spent at war within myself.

**Did being fifty mean I was old?**

**How are people around me going to view me? How am I going to view myself? How was I going to change? Was my body suddenly going to abandon me?** I did make one decision, no one had to know I was fifty. I would simply 'pretend' that I was forty-something and nothing would change. Well fifty came and as I proceeded to fifty-one and fifty-two I had gained weight before, but this was all in my stomach, and I couldn't get a handle on losing the weight. I began to notice a few gray hairs, which I immediately covered up. My hair texture began to change and those cute looks I used to love didn't seem to work well any more. Medical professionals asked different questions. Now when I went for a physical they measured me to have a base line to evaluate my 'shrinking', they talked about bone density tests, colonoscopy, and heart disease. EKG's and stress tests became part of a routine physical. No one asked any more if I was pregnant. Now when I go out and see patients they are more comfortable with me because they and/or their family feel comfortable with a mature' women.

Now I am in my sixty's and my seventy's are coming fast. I go between fear, peace, hope and despair. One day I am planning what I want in the rest of my life. The next day I am hiding from the fact that many establishments consider me as a Senior Citizen. My preconceived notion about that is, my life is over, the rest of my days will be spent at nutrition centers getting a meal once a day, until I am no longer able to go out.

I have decided that now is the time for me to become educated about Aging from a different perspective than I learned in the past. This Aging person is no longer someone **out there** that I am here to provide a service to.

## THIS AGING PERSON IS ME

I would never want to return to adolescence with changing hormones, choices about careers, partners, to have sex or not, the fear and desire for independence. I am not sure I want to return to my twenty's either. That was such a time of struggle for me. Defining values, learning skills, developing a personal identity, and discovering that my expectations about how life would work were not very realistic. My thirty's were filled with more changes, which included going back to college, living on my own, and marriage, having children, and adapting to in-laws. I was finally a real grown up with responsibilities for someone's life beside my own.

I don't really think I want to go back there either. I loved motherhood. I loved my babies. Those days are filled with very special memories. They were also filled with worries, and stresses

2

that come from juggling job and family and for me loosing any sense of myself and what I needed during that time. My forty's continued this process with family but we had the added challenge of losing parents and coping with illness of a parent, and care of the parent left behind.

So without regrets I am ready to move forward to my next challenge. This time I am armed with experience, an identity, a philosophy of life that has been tested, and motivation to really live the time I have left. I am not saying that I am not shaky about the challenge before me, but I am going to learn as much as I can about this process of Aging, I will face changes and developmental tasks one at a time. I will use all of my past learning as well as my present experience to make this part of my life as rich as the other parts. I hope that as more of us hit this mark we can acknowledge where we are, talk about life's endings, and share insights and ideas that will enrich not only us as individuals; but also society as a whole.

## DEVELOPMENTAL TASKS IN AGING

An infant who is healthy begins to move toward independence almost as soon as he/she is born. The developmental tasks of infants, toddlers, pre-school, grade school, pre-teen and teen are predictable. We know for example that the mind and mobility of a toddler is quite different than that of a third grade child. We know that what a third grade child is capable of understanding is different than a 16 year old. We don't expect a grade school child to think and behave like an adolescent; and we work with the child to help them understand that they are just not ready to deal with certain things in third grade that they will be ready to deal with at sixteen.

In Aging we **reverse** the process. We move **over time** from being independent adults capable of managing complex tasks required to live and support ourselves, to a person who often needs assistance with basic daily living activities. As we age we gradually lose our mental sharpness, understanding complex tasks becomes more difficult. Our memory for the present becomes less readily available, and details from the past seem to play a more prominent part in our daily thinking.

We often lose our energy, we need more naps, our hearing is not as sharp, and our vision becomes clouded. Our mobility, our ability to get around, take care of normal household tasks becomes more difficult. Often physical aches and pains become something we live with daily. **Our health begins to fail often in ways we didn't expect.** Our sense of touch is less dependable,

3

our experience of heat and cold is often impaired, we are more prone to falling, and if we fall, we are more likely to break something.

In childhood our world

## expands

to include friends, teachers, fellow students, and fellow workers. We move away from the family we were born into. **We become respected for our accomplishments and skills**. In aging on the other hand our **circle of our life becomes smaller**. We lose our spouses; we lose our friends either through death or severe physical or mental impairment. We often lose our connections with neighbors as the old friends we became used to, move to smaller places and new busy young people take their place. Because we lack energy we often don't make an effort to meet these new neighbors so we become more isolated in our home. If we are fortunate enough to have adult children who live close and who are able to fit some time in for us this becomes our whole world.

## Financial challenges

began to infringe on our lifestyle.

When we worked our health insurance usually paid some part of medicine expenses. When we become old we get very little help with the cost of medicine. I have seen people who are spending close to a thousand dollars a month on medications even with the new Medicare D plan. In addition we often have to pay for help with things that we used to do for ourselves, such as yard work, household repairs, and housecleaning. These things are not covered by insurance.

**The fact is that most of us imagine that we will live independently to old age and will die peacefully in our sleep without ever having to make changes in how we live.** The statistics don't support that. Most of us will **not** die in the home we worked most of our adult years to pay for, the home that is somehow an extension of how we see ourselves in this world.

**Our home represents who we have been, who we have loved, and who we are today in our heart. In our homes we are surrounded with the story of our own life and the lives of those we have loved. This story is written in every piece of furniture, every picture on the walls, the colors we choose flowers, music, and books that line our shelves. Someday, however, we will most likely be required to let go of this treasure. We will be required to**

choose which memories we will take with us, which parts of our story will surround us as we become less able to manage more complex needs and continue with the new developmental task of letting go.

So it seems that one of the major developmental tasks of aging is **learning to let go.** We need to let go of skills, abilities, privileges, health and cognitive 'sharpness'. **These tasks come at varying times for each individual** but unless we die suddenly through an accident, or sudden illness that takes us quickly we will each have to face some or all of these developmental milestones in aging. **How we deal with these losses and changes in our lives can make the difference in a life of peace and joy or a life of misery and pain.** The important thing to remember is we do have

choices

**on how we handle what comes into our lives**.

These choices can make a major difference in the quality of our lives as we continue to live through aging and finally face our own death.

My vision and hope is that in these pages we will began to ask questions, define roles, and plan for how we want to live this new stage in our lives. I for one want to live the remainder of my life with dignity, class, humor, courage, and

# Pizzazz

## OUR CULTURAL EXPERIENCE OF AGING

American Culture has often been referred to as the 'melting pot'. We publicly proclaim that many different, distinct cultures go into making this person we call American. When the chips are down we celebrate our oneness in diversity as we did after 9-11. The media projected before us an acknowledgement and celebration of many diverse heroes in the first months after the World Trade Center tragedy. We celebrated ethnic differences, the Hispanic, Oriental, African American. We celebrated our oneness from top management to cleaning people.

**These people all became connected equally and honored in a moment of madness and national mourning**. But as Americans we hold our prejudice close to our heart on a day to day basis. **We assign specific qualities to groups of people just because they belong to that group**. We make judgments about how someone will behave, how much respect they deserve, and weather they will be listened to **based on the qualities we assign to the group they belong to**. I have observed that our society tends to create

## Invisibility shields

around people or groups that evoke feelings of discomfort. We have done that with many ethnic groups over the years, and **this has created a culture of anger around the youth of these groups**.

We put these people in prisons, public housing, the inner city, just to **avoid** having to see them. **Prejudice allows us to de-humanize unique persons who experience the same longings, desires, and hurts that any other human person experiences.**

If we only see a picture in our head **that we painted** of this group then we have no responsibility to treat them with respect and compassion. **We can provide them with minimum services as a society and still go to our churches on Sunday and believe that we are righteous people**.

**The old are the fastest growing 'invisible' people in our society as we baby boomers trudge toward aging.**

We have been dehumanized often by the very people we **expect** to have more insight and understanding of the challenges we are facing each day. Physicians and other health care professionals often explain less to an older patient. They often assume that the patient will not understand the complexity of what is going on in their bodies. They speak to adult children, or other relatives or friends but **fail** to speak to the Aging patient in **a manner that the patient will understand.** In explaining procedures or tests that the patient will undergo, they often don't take the time to prepare the patient for what to expect in terms of discomfort. When they recommend a procedure to deal with a medical problem they often fail to give complete information that can be understood easily by the patient. Part of the problem here is that as we age and our hearing and vision may become impaired **it takes more time to talk to us**. The current health care industry is more interested in the **quantity** of health care provided rather than the quality. However I don't believe that is the entire explanation. When my children were younger, especially my youngest daughter. She had to undergo some frightening tests at about age ten. The nurses and Doctors

6

took a whole lot of time explaining to her what to expect with the procedure, and making sure she understood. They recognized that children **will cooperate better** if they know what to expect. If as we age we lose our mental sharpness and our ability to quickly process complex information we **deserve** to be treated with the same kindness as a child.

I believe that many in the health care field see caring for the old as **a burden** rather than a privilege. **In our weakness they see their future and we make them uncomfortable.** So they send us to nursing homes where they tell us we can get the care we need. Nursing homes, as they are run today, in my judgment are the **tenement buildings for the old**. When you move into a nursing care facility, you **lose** your physician and you get the house doctor. These physicians usually see patients in ten or more facilities. **I don't believe they see people, they see rooms, diagnosis, mindless, non-entities without feelings.** Patients are objects to be turned, income, noisy, and bothersome. We have completely floated behind **the invisible shield** when we go to a nursing facility.

I believe that being aware of what we are dealing with offers us **options** if we recognize where others are coming from. I believe we can compensate for some of our losses for a long time and get the care we need. And we can do it **graciously. However**, if we **refuse** to think about our aging and how it **affects every part of our life as we have known it, we will be unprepared to face it's challenges when we are ill and vulnerable**. We then turn over the power in our lives to someone who cares little for us as a person, and we seal the seam of the **invisible shield**.

# Family

There are genetic patterns, in our body, that we have no control over. Just as when we were a child there were genetic components that influenced how short we were, size of our hips, if we were out going or shy, our hair color, and physical skills. **We each needed to learn to live within the parameters of the genetic package we got from our parents**. As we age we are once again faced with genetic patterns. This often goes beyond some superficial things such as early graying, wrinkles, etc. We are also subject to contract diseases **that tend to run in our family**. These include such things as history of cancer, heart disease, strokes, diabetes, osteoporosis, arthritis, as well as hearing and vision problems.

**We also had examples of how the family we grew up in dealt with aging.** Did they give into every ache and pain, did they 'act' old, did they stop going out, etc. **These examples are powerful in terms of what we expect of our life as we age.**

At this time in history we are very likely live longer than our parents. **We are also likely not to have a loving family around**

to take care of us through all the stages of

aging until death,

We no longer have large extended families; both parents often work to support their family, many adult children live in different cities than their parents do. **Families are not as cohesive as they were in the past.** We have lost that sense of the flow of life, we often fail to recognize that life has a **pattern** that includes death as well as new growth.

our individual lives do have a beginning and an end !

We often cannot depend on our family, adult children, and grandchildren, to care for us as our parents did for their parents. Our adult children are frequently scattered across the country. We are a mobile society.

**To be fair,** I want to mention that we are living longer, and we can be kept alive with new drugs, advances in treating heart disease and other illnesses that would have taken our ancestors quickly. We live longer, but many times we live in poor health and need ongoing assistance to manage daily needs. **So our children aren't being neglectful they just cannot do everything.** They are often managing jobs, their own family, and many times the care or responsibility for an in law and a parent who have failing health. In my work experience **most** adult children give up a large part of their time and their life to try and help meet a parents needs and keep a parent in their home as long as possible. This is done at a sacrifice of time spent with their own family, giving up leisure, vacations, and retirement dreams. Families often continue to provide this care until they become ill, or just burn out, and can no longer cope with the demands of managing two households, and care of a sick parent.

# HEALTH

As I mentioned above new breakthroughs in medicine can keep us healthy longer, which gives us the opportunity **to live a quality life to an older age.** Worn out parts can be replaced with steel rods to keep us mobile, balloons and stints can be inserted in our vessels to keep our arteries open, Dialysis can keep our kidneys going, and respirators and inhalers can keep air in our lungs. Researchers continue to develop new technology to extend the life span.

Even with all of these breakthroughs, however, **we will die**. It may be quick or it may be slow but no doubt it will occur and we don't have a great deal of control over what illness will be our last or how it will progress.

In our society, even medical professionals often have difficulty coping with death. As a society we tend to deny death and avoid talking about our own death or the death of a loved one. We avoid talking to family about their own dying. We have not incorporated a central belief system that views life as a whole circle where both birth and death are considered a normal progression of life. We are a consumer society and often we are able to buy whatever we want. We surround ourselves with things and sometimes miss the most important and tender moments in life. This denial of our death and aging can affect our general health as well as our emotional health. We cannot deal with a reality that we will not face.

# CULTURAL NORMS

So as a society the young are held up as the standard of perfection. Aging people are not seen as a value, only as a drain on our social systems. Income and your ability to earn income are the criteria that we use to determine a persons worth and value in our society.

Nursing homes are a standard of care for the frail old. Assisted living housing is becoming a standard of care for those old who can manage some tasks of daily living but not all. Senior housing, are places that attempt to pretend that we are all active and healthy and that we want to spend our time with people our own age. **The norm is that we try to get the old out of our neighborhoods, into places where they won't inconvenience us, or remind us that there is**

9

**more to life than youth and work.** We have forgotten as a society that we are not small self-contained units that don't need anyone else to live our life in a full and meaningful manner.

It seems that all of this discussion is pretty bleak. However, I believe that it doesn't have to be a dark and dreary time in our life. I believe we have choices about how we handle these challenges. **I believe that once we recognize the reality that we live with, we can make decisions that will bring the most pleasure and meaning into our lives on a daily basis.**

# CHAPTER 2

## Choices

Elizabeth Coatsworth (who lived to be ninety-two) wrote, "Outwardly I am eighty-three years old, but inwardly I am every age, with the emotions and experience of each period. During much of my life, I was anxious to be what someone else wanted me to be. Now I have given up that struggle, I am what I am.

## Acknowledgement of Our Aging

## Old is a matter of not having died.

We have managed to stay alive a long time. This demonstrates that we have stamina, that we have been able to adapt to changes, live through difficult situations, and recover from various illnesses during our life.

It is not in our best interest to pretend that our physical abilities are the same as when we were twenty, thirty, or forty. When we refuse to acknowledge our personal reality we tend to make decisions that are not in our best interest. Sooner or later the consequences of making decisions that are not in our best long term interests will catch up, then we will often have more complex and difficult choices to make at that time.

**The interesting thing about the choices we make is there are paybacks and benefits, which result from all choices we make.**

For example, as I begin having those aches and pains that come with aging, I can choose not to go out, I can withdraw from my life because it is more difficult to get around. The results of this choice could be, in the short run I feel less pain. My family may spend more time with me initially, and those people who have been a part of my life for a long time may show me sympathy. Sometimes we can confuse this with loving behavior. On the other hand, another person may choose to continue their activities but pace himself or herself and take more rests between activities. These people have a sense of being needed by someone or something. They continue to have friends and people they interact with on a regular basis. **They also have a reason to get up every day, get dressed, and get moving.** They tend to take better care of their health. They stay connected to their community, and their family.

Do they physically feel less pain than the person who just stays home? I don't think so. I believe that often they are in pain, but the quality of their life is much richer. When they do become ill they have access to more help from friends, which doesn't put such a burden on their family. They also tend to recover more quickly from illnesses because they have a reason to push themselves so they can get back into whatever activity they are doing. I believe that as we approach our sixties or even our seventies we need to recognize that the process of aging has begun. We need to take stock of where we are today -physically and emotionally. How connected we are with family, community, church? What do we believe spiritually? What do we believe about an afterlife? Do we believe there is a Power greater than ourselves guiding us along in life.

**How am I financially? What options do I have within the financial resources that I have? Finally cognitively, how is my ability to remember, learn new tasks and think clearly?**

In order for us to make informed choices about how we want to live out this stage of our journey as human beings we must know where we are right now. This is not to cause us to feel bad about our life. It is not an opportunity to judge and blame ourselves for not taking better care of ourselves when we were younger. **We all made decisions when we were young that we would rather not think about, or that we wish would have been different.** It is easy for us to look back at our life and be critical of the decisions we made when we were younger and knew far less than we know now. **The fact is that we made those decisions based on the information we had at that time emotionally, educationally, and based on what was going on around**

12

**us.** Blame and beating ourselves up will do us no good as we go on this fact finding mission to discover **where we are at this moment** in time, and how do we want the remainder of our life to go.

So let us begin to look at our current reality based on the information we have today. This can be the jumping off point for making choices about our future. **We all know that something is going to get us eventually and we will die from whatever this disease process is.** The odds are that the diseases we are susceptible to will be something that is a genetic weakness in our family background. Some common diseases that tend to run in families are heart disease, diabetes, strokes, osteoporosis, arthritis, hearing and vision problems, Alzheimer's, and some types of cancer. We probably already know a good deal about this **pattern of illness in our family** based on what grandparents died from, what illnesses our parents had or died from, what various aunts or uncles may have died from. Because one person in our family died from a specific disease doesn't necessarily mean we are doomed to get that disease. Medical science has developed many treatments for diseases that in the past may have been life threatening or debilitating. What we are looking for is a **pattern,** that may be prevalent in our family, and which may indicate a genetic link that could affect our health in the future as we age. Knowledge is power.

## Knowledge is power

Knowing what tendencies toward specific illnesses we may have can allow us to learn ways to reduce our risk of getting this illness. We can become aware of early signs of this illness, which could help us seek medical intervention sooner. This knowledge could save our life, as well as reduce some debilitating affects that an untreated illness in its later stages can cause to our ability to function independently.

In my family heart disease and related problems was something that affected the men in our family. My grandfather on my mother's side died of heart trouble in his fifties. My Father and three of his brothers all had heart attacks in their fifties. In addition my father and each of his brothers also had surgery for aneurysms. My mother had a heart attack in her late seventies. My grandmother on my father's side had heart problems and ultimately died from a stroke. My father's sisters each developed Alzheimer's or some form of dementia. My grandmother on my mother's side had some dementia. My mother's two sisters have both had strokes. This knowledge that I have about my own families genetic weaknesses lets me know about some areas I need to consider in planning for my own future. Related to heart problems, I am working today on weight management, an exercise plan, meeting my nutritional needs, and regular screening for cholesterol. I am currently taking medication for high cholesterol. I am hoping that as I improve on my nutrition I will be able to either go off this medication or reduce the dosage. In terms of the Alzheimer's/dementia, I have already completed a living will stating what I do and do not want done if I develop this disease. My husband and I have had some discussions, about how to handle decisions if I am not capable of making decisions for myself. I am also informing both my children about my wishes for care if my care cannot be managed in the home.

Doing these things now in my sixty's doesn't **guarantee** that things will go as I plan today. But making choices today, informing my family of my wishes, making sure that I have done my part to be less of a burden on them if I should develop Alzheimer's or dementia allows me to make my own choices. I have told my children and my husband that I will **not** ask them to promise that they will not put me in a nursing home. I have seen many families where the person responsible for making a decision for another family member is tormented because they promised they would never put this person in a nursing home. The fact is there are some conditions that can only be managed at home with extreme difficulty to the person responsible for providing the care. I would like my family to consider other alternatives before placing me in a nursing home. I would like to consider some type of assisted living before going to a nursing home. And I definitely want them to know this is a choice I am making now when I am perfectly capable of making that choice. Later I may fight them depending on the kind of dementia I might develop, but they know my wishes before this happens. My hope is that making those decisions now will make it less painful in the future, for the people I care most about. We have been willing to talk about this as a possibility they may have to deal with based on the genetic patterns in my family.

In the movie Forest Gump the quote

## 'Life is like a box of chocolates, you never know what you're gonna get'

**is true**. All of our planning could be completely off and we may develop some other disease that we haven't planned for. **The fact that we have been willing to have open discussions about these issues before they become a reality in our lives will help us make better decisions at the time we have to deal with whatever comes our way.**

How is my health today? What are my current challenges? As we are taking stock of our current reality, at whatever age we are, we need to look at what is our current level of functioning. What are my current health problems? How am I coping with these health problems? How does this affect my ability to do what I want to do?

## What am I doing to take responsibility for my health today?

At this point in my life I am pretty healthy. I do find that I am more tired when I get home from work in the afternoon. Since I have started walking more and doing exercise I am more able to bend, and do what I need to do in order to take care of my home, yard, as well as my personal needs. Making a decision to work at getting to a more healthy weight has really helped me do more of the things I like to do.

My vision is more of a problem because I can no longer wear contacts and I don't like to wear glasses. I must admit that I don't do well with this problem and I usually keep my glasses in my purse **in case I need them**. I have made a decision however to wear my glasses when I am driving for safety. I have also made the decision not to drive long distances at night. My night vision has definitely diminished and **I need to be responsible** in terms of not only my safety but also the safety of others on the road with me.

Other ways I choose to take responsibility for my own health is to improve my diet and work on eating more healthy and balanced meals. I have regular screenings for high cholesterol, bone density tests to monitor for osteoporosis, and mammograms to watch for early signs of breast cancer.

I also make different decisions about what I can do and what would be better left to younger people with better balance and bones than I currently have. I learned this from caring for many older persons with broken hips, arms, etc which they got trying to do things they were no longer able to do.

One year when I was home visiting my mother she locked her key in the house. She sent me to get the ladder so she could climb in the bathroom window. As a child this was always how we got into our home if the house was locked but I never dreamed that my mother would still think that was an option at seventy-nine! I began to lecture her on possible consequences of this choice she was making. If she got dizzy or lost her balance and fell she could easily break an arm or hip. The quality of her life would diminish rapidly. My mother has always a very active and involved woman. One poor choice could have ended many things that provide her joy and meaning in her life.

This is what I'm talking about in **recognizing our present reality**. We would very much like to think we could do anything we used to do when we were younger. **But let's not wait until the accident occurs to realize that some things are better left to younger more agile people.** Let's also not be so cautious that we are afraid to live. That is not what I am talking about. I am talking about making reasonable accommodations recognizing that our abilities are not what they were twenty or thirty years ago. One fall can cause us to lose our independence and ability to do the things we enjoy doing that improves the quality of our life.

Studies have shown that many people in nursing homes are there because of a broken hip, shoulder, or wrists. These fractures were, frequently, due to them trying to do things that would have been better left to someone with better agility and balance in the first place. Some of the choices that I have seen fractures result from are: changing high light bulbs either by climbing on a chair, ladder or table, trying to trim trees using a ladder, cleaning gutters, doing strenuous yard work in the extreme heat of the day etc. Another big one is not having proper lighting on stairs or hallways at night. Often we can change an unpleasant or dangerous outcome, with a small awareness of what some of the risks are as we age. Then taking precautions that are available to avoid placing ourselves in a position of becoming seriously injured just so we can maintain our independence and not have to ask for help.

# How can I feel good about myself when my body is letting me down?

We have limited control over our physical wellness as we age, much the same as when we were children. As a child we had genetic components that influenced if we were short or tall, outgoing or shy, hair color, and physical skills. **We somehow learned to live within the parameters or limits of our abilities, and strengths, as well as our shortcomings and deficiencies.** As we grew up we developed ways to compensate for a limitation, and choose to develop our strengths and skills. We did what we liked and what we were good at. An example, would be, if we always had difficulty with math we didn't go into engineering. We can do the same process with our Aging. We can continue to choose to do the things we like to do within the limits of our health, and physical abilities. Just because I am on oxygen for example doesn't mean I can never do anything fun again. I often see people on oxygen in the grocery, at plays, in shopping malls. Yes it does take some planning and it may feel awkward at first. We may feel like everyone is looking at us. Most likely they aren't looking at us because somehow our disability causes them to feel uncomfortable. **But we can be somewhat creative in choosing to decorate our oxygen tank with a flower or bow tied around it.** We can dress well, hold our head as high as it goes and congratulate ourselves for having the guts to

# get up, get dressed, and get out.

If we are in pain from arthritis or some other chronic pain that often comes with aging. We can take our pain pill and go out to a movie, or for a walk, or to lunch. **We are most likely going to be in some kind of pain whether we remain at home or go out. If we choose to feed our spirit and do something we have always enjoyed doing, we may not notice the pain so much.** Even if we do continue to have the discomfort, we will have fed our spirit and emotionally we often feel better for having been out and living our life.

If we truly are not able to get out of the house we can make some choices to lift our spirits right there at home. I see so many people who are not able to get out of their homes sitting in front of the TV for hours on end. In my twenty plus years of doing home health care only once did I go into a home where the woman had some lovely music playing when I arrived. We saw the consequences of too much TV when our children were younger.

## They would become observers of life rather than active participants

Their cognitive skills became lazy because they were not challenged with the interaction of real life situations. I have nothing against a good TV program, or watching the news, or a ball game. **There are however other things we can do with just a little expenditure of energy that challenge our mind and keep us thinking.** We can begin to **write a family tree, even by just writing names of family members, and how they fit in with the family.** We can write about **our own life, what did we identify as the really important events, how did we cope with disappointments, losses, and changes that come to every life**.

These notes and memories can be a wonderful comfort to our children after we die that keeps us connected to them and in their hearts. Think of all those wonderful insights and lessons we tried to teach our children when they were teens that they judged, at that time, worthless and unimportant. When we write our story we can include those important lessons that we learned from living. Maybe after our death, when they are reading over what we have written, they will remember and finally say, "you know Mom or Dad wasn't so dumb after all". And finally,

17

## we all love getting in the last word.

**Writing our life story is a great way to get in the last word without someone disagreeing or telling us that it didn't really happen the way we remembered**. If we can't write due to vision problems get a cassette recorder and talk your story. I'm sure those who love you would be delighted to hear your voice from time to time when you are no longer with them. The important thing to remember is,

## we do have options and choices about how we live each day

Yes we may have to change the way we do things. We may have to make adjustments to handle increasing disabilities. But we don't have to sit in front of a screen watching mindless people tell us stories that are often uninteresting. **We can be an involved in our lives until the day we die**. We can really live and experience the moments both good and painful, because all life is a mixture and it is all meant to be experienced and lived to the fullest.

# Planning for Dependence

We have already noted that one of the main developmental tasks of aging is dealing with loss. The tasks of letting go of skills, abilities, privileges, health, and cognitive sharpness. These tasks come at varying times for each individual but unless we die suddenly through an accident, or sudden illness that takes us quickly we will each have to face some or all of these developmental milestones in aging.

When I visit patients in their homes we talk about planning for dependence. Most people I see don't even want to think about this. When I bring up the subject, their response is "well I hope it doesn't happen now, or I'll think about that when the time comes." **The problem is that when the time comes we often don't have the physical or cognitive ability to make good decisions for ourselves.** We may have had a disabling stroke, or developed Alzheimer's or some other form of dementia; which drastically affects our ability to make decisions that are in our best interest, or the best interests of those who will have to help us carry out our decisions.

18

**In my experience with sick aging persons, the ones who have discussed freely their options, who have explored what kinds of care, or help is out in the community before they need it; are the ones who get through these difficult times with the least amount of pain and turmoil.** I personally don't want to be the kind of person whose children are afraid to discuss the hard decisions that may have to be made in the future as my health declines. I believe if we get in the habit of making these discussions a part of living, and planning; then when we need it, we will at least all be comfortable with the subject. **Hopefully we will also have done some homework to know what are the real options that we have to meet our needs in an environment that will provide dignity and care at the time that we need this.** I might add that we cannot just do this once when we are sixty and let that be the end. Things change. Services change. New options become available. It is important to recheck these areas every five to ten years to keep abreast of what your choices are and let your family know your personal preferences **before** you need them.

In planning for dependence, some of the issues we need to consider are mental or cognitive functioning. **What are my choices if I become confused and unable to remember to take needed medication, cook, eat, bathe, etc.?** Since this loomed up in my own genetic back round this is something I really need to think about. What happens if I can no longer remember to go to the toilet and I soil myself? **Who will help me clean up?** What will happen if I am up wandering around the house all night because I become more anxious and fearful? Who will see that I am safe? What will happen when I am no longer safe to drive but due to my dementia, I am not aware of this? Who gets to make the decision that I am no longer safe to drive? Who gets to tell me? How do they tell me?

# Who do I trust to make decisions that are in my best interests?

Other questions to consider are **what are my expectations of my children when I become ill and need help?** Is my expectation that my adult children will take time off work to meet my needs? Is my expectation that they will sacrifice their own family needs, to meet my needs? **What are our adult children's expectations?** Do they feel any responsibility to help me? These questions are hard to look at and sometimes hard to answer when we are not in the actual situation. But thinking about them and talking about them helps us all prepare and make some decisions now that could be beneficial later. None of these questions have right or wrong answers. **This is just a way to start thinking and talking about things that do affect a fairly large percentage of aging persons at some time in their lives.** And for me I may very well have some genetic tendencies toward these diseases, and I would like my own family to have some information about it before we are faced with an illness that is difficult to cope with for both families and the person with the disease.

I want my children as adults to be able to take care of their own families first. I have been a working parent and I know how difficult that role is alone, but when you add on top of that trying to manage care for an aging parent the situation can become down right overwhelming. I would certainly hope that they would want me to be a part of their lives and the lives of my grandchildren. But I will not ask them to make promises they may not be able to keep later. And I want them to know that clearly now so when the time comes and difficult decisions have to be made they can move forward without feeling guilt as if they are abandoning me.

Other illnesses that can cause significant dependence are strokes, major heart disease, Parkinson's, hip fractures, severe arthritis, lung problems, and terminal illnesses such as cancer, ALS, or other debilitating illnesses.

So far we have been discussing illnesses that cause more extended periods of dependence and usually leading to our death. **But there are many smaller dependencies that come along before we get to the big stuff.** Preparing for these illnesses and managing our needs can be just as important as managing the big ones.

As we age we recover less quickly from ordinary illnesses that affect everyone. A cold or flu can go into pneumonia, which can in turn affect our heart and cause problems there. Once this has happened we become very weak, and often unable to manage our ordinary needs.

## How are we going to meet these short-term crises?

Can we move in with a daughter or son for a little while? Do we need to hire some help to come in a few hours a day? **Can our spouse do what is needed to help us or is he/she also ill and also in need of care?** Do we need to go to some type of Assisted Living housing for a short time, until we get stronger**? Often people who try to go home alone without any extra help end up having complications and taking even longer to recover.** These are all issues that we need to communicate about before we are in the middle of a situation trying to figure out what we are going to do. If we wait till we need all of this help to look at our options and resources, **some health professional will be making the decisions about our life instead of us and most likely we will not be happy with the consequences of that.**

Now you might wonder if I have done all of this already as I am now in my sixties. No. I am just beginning to look at the decisions that I need to make. **But I have had conversations with my husband and my children about aging and what my hopes are for my life as I age.** These are not pleasant things to consider, however, I believe that once we start talking about these issues and looking at what options we have for dealing with them, we are far ahead of most people. **The very fact of having these discussions with our family lets everyone acknowledge that**

**aging is a part of the life cycle**

**it brings with it unique challenges, and that these challenges involve the whole family system in someway.**

# Increasing Spiritual Resources

Another area, which our aging often brings to the forefront, is our spiritual beliefs, or lack of spiritual beliefs. **I have been with people who are alone, ill, and have very limited resources. Somehow these people managed to develop a powerful spiritual belief that brings them peace through out this process of aging.** Some of these people belonged to a formal church and gathered support from ministers, priests, and rabbi's. **Others simply believed in a power in this world that looked out for them and that would protect them.** The words we use to describe this part of our life don't matter. But often we begin to look at the meaning of our life inside of a larger picture, which includes a belief in some spiritual force. If we have a religious belief, or beliefs in a spiritual force it can be very comforting as we go through the losses involved in our aging. Sometimes having a spiritual outlook helps us deal with pain and death in our lives. **It helps us cope with unexplainable situations. And it can help us face our own death with more peace and hope.**

Religious beliefs can also help us feel valued and loved as a person even though society may not value us. It may be helpful to find a church community to support us in developing our spiritual awareness. Church communities besides providing support in our spiritual development can be wonderful resources to help us during these short-term illnesses where we need a little help with things like grocery shopping or a ride to the doctor. Often churches have volunteers that will visit once or twice a week that can help us feel connected to a community outside of our family.

When my father in law was dying his church support is what allowed him to remain at home to die. My mother in law was not well herself. We had young children at the time and both my husband and I worked full time. Other family members were just as stretched. We were there every day but we couldn't do many of the things that my mother in law needed help with at the time. Church members came daily and sat with him for several hours. When we needed to transport night nurses at seven in the evening and five-thirty in the morning, church members signed up for a different days and we had all week covered with no one having the burden of doing it all.

Often I have found that people are willing to use the benefit of their church support for the spiritual things in their life but they never think about other parts our church community can play in our lives. The key is we often have to ask for the help or accept it when it is offered. **We are such independent people that we still think we have to do it all on our own or have family do what is needed to help us.** Let's face it even when we were young and raising our children we needed some people outside of our family to meet some of our needs. Friends can be there for us in ways that our family, no matter how wonderful they are, can't.

When we are raising our children, and are busy about making a living we may participate in a church but often **our religious and spiritual beliefs**

## move around the edges of our life.

As we become older, we step back from the many activities we had going when we were younger. **We begin to focus more on what we believe about life, God, or whatever we want to define as our spiritual or central belief about why we are here, what is our purpose, and what comes next.**

In the past few years I have learned to make time for some form of meditation or mindfulness about my life, it's meaning, and my personal spiritual beliefs. **I find myself much more reflective about what is going on in my life.** I want to be mindful of my choices and build up a rich and fulfilling spiritual outlook and I am working on doing just that. We have a small group that meets at our home now to discuss various spiritual beliefs and values. This has allowed me to develop new friends at my church and helped me grow in my own spiritual values. As I do this I discover that I am not so rattled by crisis in my life or my family. I am more able to recognize that there is someone greater than I in charge of my life and He/She is not going to abandon me at this time. I am more aware of the people in my life that I have been privileged to live with and call my family or friends. **I am more willing to let them know that I care in ways that matter.** I was often too self-conscious when I was younger to tell someone that they really touched my heart, or that they mean a great deal to me now I can say these things more easily.

We have a **choice** about the attitude that we choose to express as we age.

## We can mope and groan all the way to the grave if we want to.
## It's our choice.

I can acknowledge that the society and cultural norms are correct and I am invisible. **I can choose to withdraw and isolate myself. I can choose to live in anger and resentment that life has treated me so poorly and that I don't have the respect and prestige I did when I was working.** I can refuse to go out of my home and be involved. **I can spend a great deal of my old age complaining about how awful it is to get old.** I have heard many times the saying you are so lucky to be young, "its hell to get old, don't do it". My response has always been that **I not real crazy about the alternative**.

I can choose to withdraw into self-absorption and fear of the future. This often leads to making choices that will take me down the path to isolation-withdrawal-and loneliness. Our behavior and choices tell the world and those around us that we agree with the implications of the invisible theory which reinforces the concept that I have no value because I am old.

**We can choose to just sit around and wait to die as our health and abilities change.** A person I knew once when he found out his cancer came back went to bed and waited to die. About two months went by and the hospice nurse came over and said well Sam, since you haven't died yet would you like to sit in a chair. He got up but was so weak that he couldn't stay long. He lived another three months. **He spent about five months in bed because in his mind he had already died and he was just waiting for his body to catch up.**

23

Another person may become demanding of their family or other caretakers. They want someone to be there to meet all of their needs so they can remain in their own home. These people assume little responsibility for managing their own health issues and wellness. **They fight with a passion against going to a nursing home, or other living arrangements that would make it easier on their family to manage their care.** They expect their adult children to drop everything to meet their needs when they get into crisis.

These persons often have the outlook that as long as they remain in their own home they can continue to pretend that nothing in their live has changed. **They expect their family to take care of them no matter what the personal hardship happens to be. These are also the people who never seem to notice the toll their choices are taking on an adult child trying to manage jobs, family, their own needs and a second household.**

**These persons have made one decision I WILL NOT LEAVE MY HOME, then they expect family, neighbors, or government agencies to take responsibility for getting their needs met so they can achieve their goal never having to move from their home.** This choice to remain in our own home long after we cannot manage the ordinary daily living activities on our own often have very negative ramifications for both us and our family. **We have in effect chosen to abdicate our responsibility for taking care of our needs as long as we are where we want to be. We have also focused so much on what we want that we neglect to consider the toll our decision is taking on those who have been assigned the task of following our plan.**

Our world shrinks to the size of a small circle. We are at the center of the circle and there are spinning balls (family, neighbors, government programs) circling us like planets around the sun. We choose not to notice how much in personal, financial, or government resources it is taking to meet our needs.

**The other alternative is to recognize that**

## Our happiness and peace is generated somewhere between our ears

**Outside events can make it more challenging to maintain that peace but it is still what we believe about ourselves and our lives that make the difference in how happy and fulfilled we are in our life.**

Making decisions that we talked about throughout this section can help. Keeping

24

connected with a network of significant friend's helps us keep joy in our lives. My mother in law at the end of her life was not able to get out. That lady however knew more about what was going on with her friends and her friend's children than anyone. She was always on the phone calling someone. Her vision was poor so she called the phone company and told them she was blind and needed help making calls and didn't want to be charged for this service. **She managed at the end of her life to keep the connections** and I truly believe that the last six months of her life were fulfilling and peaceful for her.

Going along with a positive attitude is taking responsibility for managing our own health both physically and emotionally.

## It is not someone else's job to make me happy

**It is not their job to help me feel needed, nurtured, cared for. It is my job, to be the kind of person that others want to be around. If I complain about my aches and pains whenever I am with someone else; if I am always asking them to do something for me when they are around, then I promise you they won't want to be around you for long. I need to keep my sense of humor and learn to laugh at some of the events that are occurring in my life.**

My mother one-day was getting up at night to go to the bathroom and she lost her balance and fell. Her response was to laugh and yell at my dad (who had died some years before) for not watching out for her. When she called and told me the story, we both had a great laugh. I recognized the potential seriousness of the situation and we talked about being careful. But I didn't feel the need to do anything at that moment, and she didn't get caught up in fear or anger about her own risk of injury as she aged.

Other activities that can help us keep a positive attitude are, spending time in a elementary school. Helping a child who is having a hard time with reading or some other skill have some one on one attention can be enriching for both. Spending time with your grandchildren, taking a class at a community center or local college are things that can keep you connected to life. Learning a new hobby. Something that you always thought you might like to do. Organizing your photograph albums and writing dates, and names of people in them. When I am organizing photo albums I am celebrating my own life as well as spending time with happy memories that warm my soul. Going

25

to the local library and just watching the people can be an interesting diversion, especially in the children's section. Going to senior programs can be helpful because they sometimes offer low cost trips. My personal thing is not to spend too much time just around old people. We all need diversity in our lives.

Remember how wonderful grandparents were when we were children?

**We can have a positive attitude even in the midst of heartache and pain. Any of us who have lived sixty or more years has learned to deal with pain in our lives.** We have had to have some resilience in order to have made it this long. We have had to face disappointments and heartache and we found a way through all of this. We can still do it.

I have a daughter, who has ADHD and had difficulty with attention when she was younger, which made learning a challenge. I always told her that she had to work a little harder to get what she wanted but she could still get it. I believe it is the same with our aging. **We may have to work a little harder at times to have a positive attitude but we can still do it.**

I'm not sure what people mean when they talk about the golden years. Maybe it is our understanding or expectation about what these golden years are suppose to be that gets us in trouble. When I got married I had many expectations about what my marriage was going to be that were totally off. I still can say I have a satisfying marriage. No it is not what I expected but I am married to a good man who cares about me and his children and will care about his grandchildren when they come. He cares about his family, and was a wonderful son to his parents when they became ill. We both had to make adjustments to what we expected from each other and what we got. Sometimes it was very hard and other times it was easy.

It is the same with our golden years. Our expectations may not be met but we can still continue to have a satisfying life that is filled with joy and sorrow, good times and bad times, and we can take what comes and feel good about ourselves. **No one ever promised that just because we are old we should have no problems. No one ever said that once we became old we would not have to deal with family crises, problem children or grandchildren, or any of the other issues that life brings. No one ever said that we would never have to worry about money when we got old.**

**We can do it though with joy and laughter if we choose to be positive. We are survivors; we have made it to sixty, seventy, eighty or more. We just need to keep**

making choices that will help us live the life we want to live in the midst of all the chaos and garbage that may be thrown our way.

# Remember

joy and peace is born between our ears.

## It is what we think that causes our pain most of our life

And we can make decisions about what we allow to occupy our thoughts.

# CHAPTER 3

## EMOTIONAL QUESTS

The emotional quests of aging are impressive and can be daunting. The good news is they come usually in stages, which means we don't have to deal with them all at one time. So as we look at some of the quests we will face as we age we need to remember that we are

# resilient as human beings

and we really can make it through many difficult situations and events in our lives.

If we have lived to old age we have already met many difficult situations and survived or we wouldn't be here now. We have already developed coping mechanisms. Some of them work well for us and others may need some fine tuning but we can do this aging thing with class and style.

Not perfectly because none of us are perfect. We have our personal styles, our history, and the not so pretty parts of ourselves to live with, however, we have already learned to live with ourselves. We already know a lot about how we cope, and we can continue to learn more.

**The first challange many of us often face is retirement.**

Retirement has many freeing options, but work brings with it a sense of identity, income, social contacts, and often some meaning in our lives. Some of us have planned well for retirement in terms of savings, and investments. Others have lived paycheck to paycheck and have little reserve.

**No matter which group we fall into when we receive our first Social Security check and realize that is our income for the month it is indeed a challenge.**

It can bring up old fears about security and safety. It can cause us to become so fearful about spending that we began to live as if we are in abject poverty. It can cause obsessive worry questioning if we planed well enough. Will we outlive our money or will our money outlive us? Will we be able to afford to do some of the things that we enjoyed when we were working? Will we be able to do the things we always thought we would do when we retired?

I have seen many people over the years as I have worked in the field of home health, who have become

## frozen in a state of poverty.

They have money enough to meet their needs and be comfortable, but they are terrified of not having enough. I met a couple once in their upper eighties. Both were ill and becoming more frail. They truly needed more help if they were going to try and continue living in their home. They had over one hundred thousand in savings that they could access as well as having a fairly good monthly income. They would not hire help because they thought they couldn't afford it. They were frozen in the fear that there would not be enough later when they really needed it. **How much of our lives have we spent planning for an unknown future carrying with it an unknown disaster instead of meeting today's needs and problems knowing in our heart, we would be able to cope with whatever the future presented?**

# Loss of Loved Ones.

I believe losing loved ones often catapults us into staring our own mortatility directly in the face. It causes us to look at what we believe about life, death, and the meaning of human existence. It forces us to make changes in our everyday living especially with the death of a spouse or significant other. **Every loss causes a change in our self perception.** When our parents die, for example, we become the older generation.

## We are the keeper of family values,

traditions, and teachers of wisdom to the younger generations.

When siblings begin to die we lose those people who have been connected to our very being as long as we can remember, people who often understand why we are the way we are.

Someone to share a memory with that no one else would understand. If we had a close relationship with a brother or sister it can be like losing part of yourself. I had an aunt who was the last one living out of eight children. The family was very close throughout the years, and they were both friends and family. She grieved that loss until the day she died. Her grief was based on the loss of the individual people but **also it was the loss of customs, values, and shared celebrations.** As each of us move out of our family of origin and into an adult family of our own, we give up some of the 'old' family customs and take on customs of the family or people whose lives intersect with ours.

When we lose our parents and siblings we must adapt to someone else's way of doing things in terms of family celebrations, customs.

The loss of a spouse is certainly the most life altering event's we must face. This person who we may have lived with for forty or more years. This person who for better or worse knows us more intimately than any other person. This person who often was co-creator of our children. I often liken losing a spouse to losing a body part. When a person has an amputation they have a phenomen called phantom pain. They continue to have pain in their missing limb even though it is no longer there. **This pain can last a long time, and even when it is no longer acute it can return unexpectedly**. When we lose our spouse we must learn to live alone, possibly for the first time in our lives. We must learn to do that part of daily activities that our spouse always did.

**We no longer have that person always around to bounce something off of or just to have a conversation with.**

If we are very old when this occurs we may have to deal with children wanting us to move from our home. We may not be able to manage all of our needs alone and we have to make some big decisions about how we will handle the things we can't do. In addition we might lose half of our monthly income. The widow/widower gets to keep the larger Social Security amount between husband and wife. This can have a major impact on how we are able to manage monthly expenses.

**So how do people cope with these losses of loved ones?**

In my experience, the coping of individuals facing loss of loved ones is as varied as are the people. The ones who seem the most peaceful and content have several things in common.

1. **A spiritual base of some kind.** A belief that there is more to life than this present moment, that there is a higher force and that somehow we will continue to be connected even in death.

2. **A family support system.** Children or grandchildren who keep them connected to life and give them a reason to get up every day.

3. **They use their positive memories to enhance their life now.** Memories that warm their heart whenever they think about the person no longer here.

4. **Something to do** whether it is volunteering for a favorite agency, helping a neighbor, helping with the care of a grandchild, or writing a family history, or personal memoirs.

**What I am talking about is a reason to get up and get dressed every day.**

My father died at sixty-nine years old, about six months before he planned to retire. His death was sudden. My mother's main coping mechanism was taking on the widows in her neighborhood. She provided rides to people all the time. She became more involved in church clubs, and offered to help my sister who was a single parent with her son when she worked and went to school. Now she is no longer an officer in the clubs she belongs to, but she still helps out serving food at soup kitchens, she still helps out with a grandchild for my brother, she also goes around the country and visits other grandchildren. There are times she still feels sad about my father not being here for some event. But she sits with it when the sad feelings come for only a little while then she moves on to living her life as best she can.

# Loss of Health and Abilities

As we age we certainly lose some of the edge we had when we are younger. We get aches and pains we never had before. Our hearing and vision may become diminished. When we get sick, it usually takes longer for us to recover. We may find ourselves worrying that we will get some **"family" illness**, for example, if a brother or sister died from a stroke we may fear having a stroke. We also become very aware that any illness can escalate into the one that causes our death. We may wonder who will be there for us when we become ill.

Most people are not so much afraid of dying as they are fearful of pain and disability. As we see our friends and loved ones become ill and die, our fears can overwhelm us; or we can go into a state of denial that this could ever happen to us. I believe that the manner in which we deal with our health issues and losses has a great deal to do with our sense of contentment and peace in our lives.

As we age it takes a lot of effort to stay well. Actually our defination of well also changes. In my twenties if I had bad menstrual cramps I took that as a reason to spend a day in bed. Now, I am working on knowing which aches and pains are part of my life from here on, and which ones need some medical consultation.

## Inactivity

can cause more disability than the actual illness causes.

I hate to keep using my wonderful mother as an example but Pauline is an amazing women. At this writing she is eighty-seven. She has had two knee replacements, she has had a heart attack, quadruple by-pass, she has some arthritis in her shoulder, she has chronic digestive problems, and some chronic bladder infections. The point is she is raerly out of pain or without some kind of discomfort. Her theory is, **if I stop I'm doomed.** To a great extent she is right. Pauline never misses a family party, a trip, a church dinner, or a meeting. My aunt, my dad's youngest sister, was the same way. She became more frail and had difficulty walking, but she always showed up at family parties. She was also always bugging my uncle to plan another trip, because she loved to travel.

On the other hand, I have seen people who when they found out that they had a chronic or terminal illness just sat down and waited to die. This often occurs with lung problems, because it takes such an effort to keep moving. A woman I know just stopped doing one thing after another because it was hard or uncomfortable. Within a year she had become so frail that she could hardly walk. She ate poorly,and she was often too sick to come out for family gatherings. She spent her days in front of the TV hoping that someone would come to visit her. When people came she would say things like old age is hell. **Who wanted to be there?**

When a man I knew found out his cancer had come back, he went to bed to wait for his death. It took him five months to die. I wonder if his life in those five months could have had more quality if he would not have spent them in bed.

The point of this discussion is that as we age we need to push ourselves in order to continue functioning.

## Healthy has a different meaning than it did when we were young.

and if we can adapt our lifestyle to these different changes, we can continue to feel connected and have a meaningful life.

## Loss of Independence.

How will we deal with our life when we can no longer drive?

What will we do when our children or doctor tell us that we are no longer safe to live alone?

What will we do when we can no longer do the basic self care things like bathing, going to the bathroom, or preparing our meals?

**How will we treat the people who are trying to help us at this time in our life?**

## We Americans have almost made a god of independence.

We make heroes of the people who made it through life without ever having to ask anyone for help. Suddenly (or not so suddenly) we are old, we are frail, and we know we can no longer manage alone.

**Do we graciously allow others to do things for us?**

**Do we thank people when they do something thoughtful?**

**Do we become demanding and inconsiderate of the time and effort someone is spending trying to help us?**

**And finally do we do as much as we can for ourselves?**

I don't know about you but I have spent a lot of my life walking a fine line between conflicting needs. How do I guide my children without being controlling, how do I love my spouse without losing myself, how do I handle being accountable at work and have a life outside of work? How do I express myself and at the same time respect someone else's right to express themself? This is no different than what we have done throughout our lives in various areas of interaction.

**Somewhere along the line, however, many people get the idea that when they became old, they should no longer have relationship problems because others should cater to their needs.**

Another common misperception is at my age I shouldn't have to worry about money.

**I don't quite know where we got the idea that we had certain rights that come with age, which somehow allowed us to bypass normal challenges involved in human interaction, good manners, and self care.** As far as I can tell the only problem we will not have in old age (and this only goes for women) is an unexpected pregnancy. Pretty much everything else is up for grabs for us, just like it is for anyone else.

## Our final loss is that of life itself

I see death as our final task in this lifetime. A final letting go to make room for other generations, new ideas, and continuation of the human race. **We all know it is before us.**

## We all know that we will walk that road

## and we will walk it alone.

How we come to our own end is often based on how we came to ends all through our lives.

**How well have we said good bye?**

How well have we prepared spiritually for this moment? Did we take the time during our aging years to repair damaged relationships? I believe that if I can come to the end of my own life and look back and say, **"I wasn't always right but I did the best I could at the time"**, then I will **find peace.**

I do know that if I have the time to know that I am in the dying process I want to say good bye well. **I want the people who mean the most to me to know the value they have had in my life.** I want them to know that I always loved them even when it seemed that I didn't. I want to have a place that is special in their heart, a place that they will honor and experience warm memories when they visit that place after I am gone. I want my funeral to be a real celebration of my life, my beliefs, my God, and making it to the other side. I hope that those who knew me well can say that I had a wonderful life and that I did my best to live it as fully as I could each day. I want them to be able to say I was willing to take risks, fail, make mistakes, and get up again. I want them to say I was a woman of honor, and that I honored my God, myself, and the people with whom I was privileged to live work, and share family bonds with.

I know that if I want that at the end of my life the way I get it is by living my present moments in a state of mindfulness now. **It will do me no good to fill my present moments with regrets about the past or fears about the future. neither belong to me.**

**Remember the poem, when I'm old I'll wear purple? Don't wait because if you don't wear it today you won't wear it then!**

# Chapter 4

## COPING STRATIGIES

I have spent quite a bit of time on looking at the challenges, losses, and changes we will each have to face as we age. Some may choose to put down this book right now and say "I'm not going to think about this right now...I'll do it tomorrow". Being a good southern woman I call that the Scarlett O'Hara Syndrome. "Remember Gone with the Wind?"

**Our generation has had opportunities that our ancestors didn't have.** We have computers, we have access to literary work from all over the world, we have to some extent been a rather 'self absorbed' generation. We have had more therapy, more self-help books, more spiritually enlightened mentors, and more time to explore the higher values in life rather than just the survival tasks that our ancestors dealt with. The opportunities for personal growth, planning, and choosing how we want to live are staggering. And because of **our shear numbers,** the opportunities to influence future generations are significant. **I believe our styles of aging will be as unique as our style of living, parenting, and working**. I also believe that

## "Knowledge is Power".

Knowing something about the process of aging, knowing something about how we cope with change, difficulties, intimacy, and friends, will help us be aware of the choices we have. And we very well may come up with some choices that no one has thought about yet.

So what are some of the ways people cope with whatever is going on in life? I am going to cite both positive and negative coping, although I recognize that this is a judgment call. What one person may identify as positive, another may view as negative. **Each of us needs to be our own judge of what feels right to us in a specific situation.** If one way doesn't work for us, that is, we don't feel a sense of peace and wholeness in our life, then we are free to choose another way to cope.

**We don't have to be stuck with old patterns of behavior that don't work unless that is what we choose.**

Some people prefer to live their lives as they always have because they like the predictability and they desperately need to feel a sense of control over the events coming into their life. Of course we are all aware that we have limited control over anything in life, and just when we get one phase of development, one job, one kid figured out, something changes and we have to start all over. We all know people who have managed to live in a small circle in which they are able to control many aspects of their life.

Some of the ways **people use control to cope** with their Aging is **isolation**. They don't go out much. They remain independent and do for themselves. What they can't do doesn't get done. They tend not to make efforts toward reconcilliation with either family or friends whom they have offended in the past. They know where they stand with this person and don't want to put out the effort or energy to change these relationships. **They feel safe and secure in their small circle of life, and they know what to expect because they avoid any situation that they don't know.**

One of the down sides of this coping mechinisism is, often as illness comes, these people are very lonely. These are the people I see who fall in their homes and lie on the floor for hours or days because no one checks on them. Or the people who refuse to look at any alternative living situation even when they truly know they are not able to meet their needs any longer in their home. These are often the people who are neglected in hospitals as well as nursing homes because there is no one to speak in their behalf. These are also the people who may have a neighbor, state worker, or attorney present at their funeral only because they have been paid to do the job.

## communication and staying connected

are vital coping skills we need as we age. We truly need to make the effort to keep in touch with other people whether it is family, friends, church, or other support groups. I will not choose to be one of the invisible aged in our society. If I remain connected and keep communicating with people I won't be invisible. I will also have access to help if I become ill and need a little help up the road.

Another part of this communication thing is being

**flexible.**

Lets face it, we are losing our peers and regular support system.  We had better be flexible enough to meet new people and develop new friendships.

I know that making friends is hard for some of us even when we were young. Our energy to reach out now, when we are old is lower, it takes much more effort to develop new friendships. **Our new relationships are not going to be the same as the old ones**; however, they can still increase our sense of being connected to living and increase our feeling of knowing that someone cares. These new people only have known us as old, they only see one dimension of our life and at times this can cause us to feel a sense of loneliness. Part of developing new friendships at any age is

# sharing stories

Thats where we find connections and joy between people. We all love to talk about ourselves so here is a perfect arena to do that, talking to someone who hasn't heard the same story a hundred times already.

Another benefit of staying connected and developing new friendships is it takes the burden off of our children to be everything for us.  Some people expect their children to be their personal shopper, chauffueur, nurse, friend, housekeeper, laundry person, and cook. Usually it is one family member who somehow gets this job, whether it is assigned by age, distance, or just goodwill.  No one can be everything to any of us.

**We need to be responsible for our own social connections and they can't all be our family**.

One of the saddest things I come across is when I visit someone and ask them who supports them, who calls to check on them, who can they count on and they reply 'no one'. No church, no friends, often no family who live in town. New neighbors moved into the neighborhood and they made no effort to meet them. They have certaintly elimanited many options for managing decreasing abilities and increasing needs. Some of these people try to **blame** their state of isolation on young people who 'don't care anymore about anyone but themselves'. I don't agree with that.

**Young people with young families are busy, but they need someone to see and care about them just as much as we do.** My daughter when she was only five loved going to visit with an older neighbor. As my daughter grew she would say "I think I'll check on Nancy because she doesn't have anyone in town." They would visit and play silly games and it was good for both of them. **And what young mother wouldn't give anything to have an older neighbor offer to watch a young child to give the Mom a break.**

Sometimes making an effort just to bring over a batch of cookies to a new neighbor and to introduce ourselves is all it takes to let them know we want to stay connected and want them to be a part of the neighborhood. With todays mobile society you could be the only grandparent that *child* has.

When my daughters were little, they began visiting an older couple up at the corner. They are delightful people, and if they need anything any of us are thrilled to have the opportunity to help. They even came to a high school play my older daughter was in. They have become like second grandparents to my daughters, especially the youngest, and it has been a blessing for us all.

# Memories

What a gift our memories are to us as we age. I came across an anonymous story on the internet about a ninty-five year old woman who was entering a nursing home. She was very positive and kept thanking the person taking her to her room. When the staff member questioned her about how she could be so sure she would be happy there the woman replied,

**"I discovered a long time ago that happiness occurs between your ears not in outside circumstances. I have wonderful memories that will fill my heart with warmth and I know I can be home anywhere."**

What an awesome attitude. I spend a lot of time now organizing my photographs so I can enjoy looking back on different stages of my life; so many things I have already forgotten. I want to keep those memories of the good times alive and in good condition so when maybe my vision not as good as it used to be I **can look inside and see and experience those moments again and find the joy I had right in my heart.**

Many of us fear Alzhiemiers, the ultimate thief when it comes to memories. There are books coming out now, that give us some ideas on how to stall and possibly prevent this dreaded disease. I certainly want to enjoy and benefit from those wonderful memories I have now. I am not willing to wait until I become "really" old to review my memories because I don't know that I will have them. **Now is the time to build this treasure resource in my heart.**

# Pleasure Laughter Music

Another coping skill is filling our life with as much pleasure as we can each day. It may be the pleasure of **watching a sunrise**, or sitting outside in the warm spring sunshine listening to the birds chatter and sing, planting a garden, taking a walk, listening to music, watching the neighborhood children play.

**Whatever it is that gives you pleasure in your life make sure you have lots of it.**

Sure we have our aches and pains, our worries, but if we add a **dash of pleasure** to the mix it improves the quality of our life today. Then if someone drops by and says, "Hi How are you doing today," you can tell them about the sunrise, the birds, the children rather than complaining about your aches and pains. The aches and pains will be there whether you sit and stare at the TV or get up and do something interesting, so you might as well do something interesting while you can.

**Laughter is major. If the normal adult population doesn't laugh enough then the aging population is often starved for good cleansing laughter. I want to began gathering comics that cause me to laugh.** I want to read stories that will increase my laughter.

My mom once fell in her home when she was getting up to go to the bathroom at night. As she was telling me about it she started laughing. I was somewhat alarmed and concerned about her being hurt. She said that when she fell, she first got mad at my dad (who had been dead a number of years) for not looking out for her and then she just got the 'giggles' at how outragous her situation was at that moment. Maybe that is why she didn't get hurt when she fell. I don't know but we both enjoyed the story and I still smile when I think of it.

This could have been a situation that got discussed as being awful and frightening, but instead she laughed at herself and went on to continue living her life just the way she wanted to.

I know that I have not had enough music in my life recently. Kids watching TV, work, and other things seem to take over and I often forget to put on some music.

When I was younger music was my life line. I played guitar and sang all the time. I am working on getting music back in my life because it brings me such joy and increases my energy by a thousand times.

I can face anything with music.

# Acknowledging our losses and using resources

Recognizing increasing limitations and using resources available are major parts of taking responsibility for our own happiness and our own lives. As we age I see so many people who just allow someone else to come in and take over things that these individuals could manage to do for themselves, things that are really important to the quality of our lives and our health.

Examples of this abound but let's look at just a few. My hearing is getting bad I notice it and ignore it. I expect others to accommodate me, rather than making the effort to be responsible for myself. So I refuse to get a hearing aide. Maybe I don't want to spend the money, maybe I don't like the way they look, or maybe it brings the reality of my own aging way too close. In the meantime I expect people around me to make sure I understand what they are saying, I allow someone else to tell me whatever it is the health professionals are trying to tell me, I tune out anything that causes me discomfort.

I become more aware of sudden memory lapses. I try to cover this up and 'pretend' that it doesn't exist. I continue to drive even though I know that I am slowing down and not quite as sharp as I was even a year ago. I am willing to put others as well as myself at risk because I don't want to be inconvienced by having to do things on someone else's time schedule.

I know that I don't have the energy to prepare meals anymore but I lie to concerned people and act like everything is just fine. I cannot explain the reason, but I do know that one very significant influence on our mental functioning as we age is good nutrition. I have seen people who were otherwise fairly healthy become very confused and unable to process information or follow directions just from poor nutrition. When you get them into a place where they are getting regular meals their thinking clears up.

Taking medication is another big one. If we find that we are having more difficulty managing to take the medication we need then we need to discuss this with someone. Sometimes if we lose a little piece of our independence and we allow someone to provide just a little help, then we can continue to  function at a higher level and have a better quality of life.

# GOOD MANNERS

Good manners never go out of style. We have rights in our life. We don't have the right however to some special treatment or indentered servant treatment from our adult children. That doesn't mean that if our children offer to do something to help us we don't accept the help. We need to remember to acknowledge that we appreciate their help and say thank you. **We need to take responsibility for what we are able to do.**

We need to be considerate of the time it takes to provide assistance to keep us in our own home. If we are aware that our adult child is spending a large amount of time helping us to remain in our home and get our needs met, maybe it is time for us to consider moving to some place where we can get help. Or we can arrange to hire in some of the things that this child or our family is doing for us. I have seen situations where adult children have all but given up their own personal life, and responsibilities in order to meet the wishes of a parent who wants to remain in their own home.

We were the first generation who has had to deal with aging parents and children still at home who needed you there.  Families are smaller and more mobile.

We no longer have large extended families to share the burden of caring for an elderly family member and allowing them to remain in their home to die. Yes some of us may be lucky to have a spouse still living and healthy enough to meet our needs in the home until we die. But the spouse who is left will have to find other resources to manage their needs. You may think that this isn't fair. You gave up your time and energy to care for someone and allow them to die in their own home and now you have to move either to assisted living or to a nursing home when it is your turn. **It may not be fair but is is real**. And it is up to us to make those decisions if we want to have some say in where we go.

# Spiritual Base

Finally I believe that good coping includes some type of spiritual belief system. We each need to see that life is more than we see in this moment. I could not have made it through my own life thus far without some spiritual values to get me through the hard stuff that was unfair and didn't make sense. **It really isn't so important as to what our Spiritual Base is, but I truly believe that we will need some connection to a larger experience than this world has to offer if we are going to make it through this last lap of our journey with dignity and class.** I would encourage you to consider either reading or visiting different churches to find something that fits for you. It may bring peace into our lives and inspires us to see events from a larger perspective.  And most of all it provides a sense of comfort in the really hard times.

For me the concept that there is a God and He/She cares for me, created me, and is waiting for me to return to the Arms of Love is very comforting. The idea that I am indeed a child of the universe and that the universe and life itself is meaningful beyond this moment, provides me with the courage to move on in difficult times.

**Knowing that there is a purpose for which I was born, and for which I remain in this world, helps me be on the lookout for opportunities of service however I can preform it. It reduces my moments of self pity and whining about the things that have disappointed me in my life.**

**Finally meditation**, being still with my own soul or essence, or center helps me live more in this moment.

# We only have moments

We have learned this over and over through out our lives. Now we really need to practice living those moments because they are so much more precious than we ever knew when we were younger. One of my favorite reminders of this point of precious moments is a line from one of the songs in the Broadway Play *Pippin*

**"....when you are as old as I my dear**
**and I hope that you never are...**
**you will sit all alone  and sequester**
**a drop of your precious youth...**
**for when your best days are yester**
**the rest are twice as dear."**

Our best days are most likely yester, but the days to come can be meaningful, and filled with love, meaning, and adventure if we will take care of ourselves and **allow the wonder of every moment to be present in our awareness**.

I know that there are more rivers to cross, and more mountains to climb, but I want to be there in awareness of it all. I missed a lot of wonderful moments in my life when I was filled with worry, anger, and regret.  I also have treasured memories of the times that I stayed in the present and experienced the life that was offered that day. I want more of that as I age. I want more moments of living my full humannes, feeling all the emotions there are to feel both the awesome ones and the uncomfortable ones.

I believe I can do it. I am becoming more ready each day to face the challenges that I meet as well as experience the wonderful emotions that are part of every life.
**I also believe that as a generation we can make a difference in how society perceives its old, and**

**that my friends, will be a blessing for all.**

# Chapter 5

## AGING MENTORS

Who are our heroes in aging? Who provided us with examples of aging with grace and style? What are our early memories of aging?

## Hero's In Society

To understand what our beliefs and values are related to our own aging we need to understand who our role models are. Then we can decide if we want to follow that path or choose another.

Does Society provide us with heroes who are old? Some, but these are very scarce. In some ways Ronald Regan was a hero in aging. He was seventy-two when elected President. We celebrated with George Burns as he continued to make movies well into his nineties.

## Aging patterns in our families

In my own family my dad's mother always seemed old. She was bent over, hair in a bun at the back of her head, well-constructed sensible shoes. When I look at pictures of her now and realize that she was my age in those days, I am amazed. However, looks don't necessarily present the whole picture. Grandma continued to work in the small grocery store she owned well into her seventies, she continued cooking, ironing, and running her large family. (In Italian families, mama runs things even after the children are grown). The point is this woman, an immigrant raised eight children as a single parent after she was widowed. She stayed connected to life, she didn't let pain get her down. She continued going to church and keeping her spiritual connection as well as her connection to her family. Parties and celebrations were always at her home.She was always a part of family functions. In her later years she needed more help to walk and get around; but she always got up and got dressed. She died at eighty-two, two weeks after having a stroke.

My other Grandmother developed dementia in her late seventies. She worked as a saleswoman in a department store until she was sixty-five. She also took care of her brother in law who lived with her. She got up and got dressed each day. My mother was her caregiver until she could no longer manage all of her daily needs. As this grandmother aged, she tended to be very isolated except for our family. She cried easily and missed my grandfather although he had died many years before. When she went into a nursing home she stopped talking. We think she may have gotten angry with her family for putting her there and then from lack of use she forgot how to talk. She lived in a nursing home for nine years and died at the age of ninety-two.

My great uncle looked like he was hundred ever since I can remember. He was an alcoholic---slept in a dark musty room. His activity that I remember was walking to the local bar and staggering home.

Other aunts and uncles aged in various ways. **What I remember was they stayed connected to family and life**. They took care of each other.

My dad did not take very good care of his physical health, but he loved traveling and he was ready for a trip any chance he had. He continued working until his death at sixty-nine. He never viewed himself as 'old' and incapable of whatever it was he wanted to do. **He seemed to take life as it came each day doing the things he loved.**

My mother's aging has been awesome. She and my dad were very active in church groups. When my dad died my Mother took on the widows in New Orleans. She would drive them places and she continued her work with her church.

She was a local community organizer in her aging years. She was president of the Ladies of Charity for many years until she resigned at eighty-two. She continues to be a part of this group helping with fundraising, caring for the poor, and doing whatever is needed. She also continues driving the "old folks" to the doctor, grocery, and other fun activities.

She helped care for her grandchildren when my sister and brother had to work and had young children. She loves to travel. After her heart attack when she was eighty she became more fearful about her health but it didn't stop her activities. She never wants to be left out of any family activities or any trips. She dresses well, uses makeup, takes care of her home, and plants her gardens. She is often in pain but this doesn't slow her down. She has suffered many losses and disappointments in her life, and I believe she has handled these losses with grace.

**I believe my mother developed her gifts through loss and loneliness in her life. She has been an example and inspiration to me as she has aged.**

# OTHER AGING MENTORS

Our families are not the only aging mentors we experience in life. Along the way, I have met many wonderful people who have provided me with inspiration as I watched how they aged. Some were persons I considered close friends and others were **just people I met along the road who lifted my spirits and brought laughter and hope into my life just being in their presence.** We have all encountered these people but often we miss their gift because we are too busy. Sometimes, however, if we allow ourselves some reflective time, we can remember these people and identify what it was about them that brought us inspiration and joy.

Some of the people who passed through my life and brought me these wonderful lessons in aging:

Carmie was a Daughter of Charity. She was a lovely Sister who spent her life in an orphanage caring for rejected children. I met Carmie in her eighties. She had a twinkle in her eyes and a dancing spring in her step. She kept up with "her boys" and remained a part of their lives until her death at ninety-two.

Then there was Gert. She lost her vision, her leg, had severe diabetes, but she never lost her sense of humor. She was also a Daughter of Charity and she stayed connected to life by helping tutor children with learning disabilities. She loved singing and talking and the St. Louis Cardinals. She may have had some down days but she never let her losses dampen her spirit.

Laura was a woman with a beautiful spirit. She was a gentle but joyous woman. I met Laura when she was dying of breast cancer. Every time I visited Laura she had a smile and words of hope and news of what was going on with her family. She never complained about the pain she experienced. Laura's husband was a Minister and she loved gospel music. Shortly before she died I went to her home with my guitar and we sang every gospel song we knew. **Her focus was on the joy of the moment and the wonderful things in her life**. She knew she had losses, regrets, and that she was losing her battle with death, but she focused on the present and the love of her husband and friends. It has been over thirty years since Laura died. I only knew her in the last six months of her life. She was not educated, wealthy, or especially gifted in ways that society would notice. The memory of Laura still warms my heart when I think of her, she was truly a gift in my life.

Verdella was a little woman who lived in two rooms with limited heating in the winter. She had a stroke and had difficulty getting around. She had no family and no friends, only the nurses who came weekly to set up her medicine. But **Verdella was full of laughter and stories of how she managed to live her life.** She didn't spend her days complaining, about how badly her life ended up. She took her lot in life and faced it with a positive spirit and was grateful for the people who came in to assist her in her final days.

These are the mentors that remind me that aging with grace and style is not about how much money I have, how many family members are still living and involved in my life, or what the status of my health is at the current moment. **Aging with grace and style is about how we approach living, it is about joy in our heart, it is about cherished memories, and finding meaning and hope in moments. It is about getting up, getting dressed, and getting moving.**

How we identify our aging mentors is not important. We can find these mentors in literature, art, neighborhoods, grocery stores, libraries, wherever people gather. We can find them learning swing dancing, working at senior centers, visiting hospitals, doing all kinds of volunteer work. George Burns, Grandma Moses, Jessica Tandy, and Kathryn Hepburn are a few people who followed their passions well into old age.

Why are aging mentors important?

# I believe that we need heroes at every stage of our lives

It gives us something to work toward. **It provides us with a dream of what could be.** It offers many different ways to approach this thing called aging. There is no perfect way to move into this phase of life. We each come with our own unique personality. We will not all be able to work right up till the end of our lives.

**What Mentors do for us is provide us with a vision and options that we can consider as we face our own aging.**

I see it kind of like when we were young, trying to find the job that was the right fit for us. We looked at other people in the field we were interested in and made some decisions about our own life based on what we saw in them. Then we took what fit for us and made it a part of our life experience, what didn't fit we let go.

Everything we see someone else do isn't going to fit for us. **The really important thing is that we can choose who we want to be as we age.** We have more choices now than our own ancestors had. By the time we are in our sixties, seventies and more, we don't have the need to impress others in the same way we did when we were young. **We are usually more comfortable in our own skin** (after all we have been in this skin for a long long time). We know more about what we like and what we don't like. **The point of looking around is not to change our whole personality or our whole approach to life. It us just to broaden our perspective and allow us to recognize that we never lose our ability to choose how we want to experience our life.**

## We can also choose not to choose.

We can allow events to push and pull us along.

Maybe we have always allowed events to control our happiness and it is too much effort to change this pattern. **That too is a choice,** but if we want more for the final chapter of our lives we can look to those mentors all around us and decide if maybe we can try changing one thing that will increase the joy of our aging and allow this time of our life to have value and meaning for us and possibly for those we encounter along the way. **We now are the Aging Mentors for the generation behind us,.**

51

# CHAPTER 6

## CHOOSING HAPPINESS

**Happiness is something you decide on
ahead of time.  Whether I like where
I am living or not doesn't depend on
how the furniture is arranged,
It's how I arrange my mind.
Annonomous from a women in her 90's
entering a Nursing Home**

**Every morning when we awaken we make a decision about how our day will go.**

We may not be aware that we are making this decision but we are making it nonetheless. We can choose to spend the day in bed recounting the difficulties we now have with the parts of our body that no longer work as we would wish. We can spend the day thinking about the people who are not there for us. We can spend the remainder of our days wishing that things were different. **But wishing won't make it so**. We make our decisions on how to make our personal wishes and dreams come true.

## Each day is a gift.

As long as I wake up in the morning, am breathing, and I can move some of my body parts without pain **I have a choice**. Even if I can't move my body parts I have a choice on how I will live out this part of my life.

In the book *Tuesdays With Morrie* the author questions Morrie about feeling sorry for himself as his body each day becomes weaker from the ravages of ALS. Morrie said **"I allow myself about fifteen  minutes a day to feel sorry for myself**. During that time I can cry for my losses, and wollow in my misery. **When the fifteen minutes are up I move on to be present to what gifts this day has to offer."**

In some ways I look at old age like a **bank account**. We make deposits throughout our lives. We make deposits of happiness, love, pleasure, education, our view of the world, spirituality, and the friendships and family connections that we nurtured throughout our adult life. In our old age we get to make **withdrawals** from this account in terms of memories, ongoing family connections, community involvement, and our basic spiritual beliefs about life, illness, and death.

We have also created some **liabilities** in this bank account, such as, anger we have carried from past hurts, failures, disappointments, and betrayals. **Depending on how we have dealt with these liabilities we may end up facing old age in the red.** On the other hand as long as we are breathing human beings **we can shift the balance**. We simply must change the pattern of our deposits into the bank account of our life.

## We do have choices.

We are not victims of aging any more than we are victims of any other stage in our life's journey. **We can choose to live in the sludge of self pity and misery** –we can stay in bed or sit in a chair until our body withers from lack of use. We can spend the valuable time with either family or friends complaining and whining about our ailments and fears. **Or we can make the choice to find something interesting in what others are doing.** We can share in the joy of our families and grandchildren. **We can find our own interests and pursue them at our own pace so that we have more to share with others than our latest pain or ailment.**

I have met many people along the way who have said; "Don't ever get old honey old age is hell". Well pardon me, but I'm not ready for the alternative yet. **I don't want to be one of those people who die to life long before their heart stops beating**.

When my body began to grow more plump after I reached menopause, I looked at myself and I could feel my shoulders sagging more, and my body looking older than I cared to look at that time. I was in my early fifties. I decided that I didn't want to go in the direction that it seemed my body was taking me. So I looked around to see what was available to help me 'spark' up my life so to speak. The first thing I did was look at my wardrobe. Just because I was overweight didn't mean I had to look sloppy and always wear dark and non descript clothes. I went shopping and **started looking for options of clothing that made me feel more alive.** I chose colors that were bright and styles that minimized the deficits that were present in my body. I wore jewelry that was bodacious and fun, I got a new hair style and started wearing glitter in my hair. Not only did I enjoy my make over process, but people are always making positive comments about how I dress and how I present myself. I wear cool hats when I feel like it, I wear heels to give me height since I am shrinking some, and when I walk out of the door I feel good about myself.

Oh, I do have other options to deal with my changing body image. I could lose weight and at some point I hope to do that. But until I am ready to cross that bridge **I can still have a positive experience of my body and how I present my self to the world. Life at any age is made up of the ebb and flow of joy and sadness, losses and gains, positive and negative.**

## The whole point is to live each moment

as it unfolds in a way that brings joy to our heart, a sense of purpose to those moments, and to fill our memory bank with positive deposits from which we can draw strength in the dark times.

# Expectations

Often it seems we expect that everything will stay the same as it is today until we die quietly in our own bed, in our own home, surrounded by those people who mean the most to us. It is amazing how many people I see in health care that comment, I never thought this would happen to me.

How many times in our lives have our rigid expectations about how things were "supposed to be" gotten us in trouble over the years? Rigid expectations revolving around any life circumstances are definitely counter productive.

I expected my husband to love and cherish me in certain ways when we married. I failed to consider that he had his own style and his own family dynamics that he brought into our relationship. I spent many unhappy years trying to convince him that his way was wrong and my way was right. **Being right is definitely not all it is cracked up to be.** We lost many years of happiness because we did not recognize the love that each of us was attempting to give the other. My own expectations caused me to make negative judgments about him and to become critical and unpleasant to be around. I often allowed anger and disappointment to simmer and fester and thus ruined many moments that could have been filled with happiness.

I did similar things in regard to my children. I expected my children to be healthy, physically and emotionally. I expected that they would pass smoothly through all the childhood challenges. I expected that my husband and I would always agree on how we parented. I expected to have happy well adjusted children who loved each other and always demonstrated that love in a positive way.

I got two children with very different personalities. Both had ADD. One had a major eating disorder and was hospitalized several times for this. The other has a very strong personality with many anger issues. My husband and I had totally different styles of parenting, this caused much pain in our lives along the way.

**I would have been so much happier in those years had I been more flexible, had I lived in the moment more.** I would have experienced much more peace and joy in my life if I wouldn't have been focusing so much on what wasn't right about me or my family. This was all about expectations and judgments. **It was about not making the choice to be happy with who the people in my life really were and celebrating the positive things we all had going for us. I often missed the beauty and unique gifts they brought into my life because I was so focused on changing the things about them that I didn't especially like.**

We all have our regreats that we bring to aging. One of the gifts of aging is that we can make peace with people we have hurt in the past. We can also choose to live the next part of our life in this world with an outlook and approach to living that will be more rewarding. We can recognize that we did the best we could with the knowledge we had a the time. **The past is past. Today is a fresh new day. We can choose to see the glitter, the sparkle in life and in the people we are privileged to have as a part of our life.**

We can choose to stay away from the people who drag us down. After living fifty to sixty or more years we often have finally learned that **the people who surround us do have an impact on our happiness.** We can choose to surround ourselves with people who **sparkle and bubble with laughter**. We no longer have to wait for someone's approval to do something. We can do what we want alone or find people with similar interests. Many college campuses have programs that offer short focused classes for older adults. This is especially true of community colleges. Many cities have senior programs that offer activities, trips, and classes of various types.

We are aging in a truly exciting time and many of our

## options are as large as we want them to be

The things we are talking about here are my dreams and vision for my aging. **I must admit that there are days that I may choose to sit in the sludge of self pity. There are still some days when I miss the mark of reflecting back the beauty and value I see in those around me. There are days when my old controlling self is out in full force. Each day I keep working at not staying there. I also work on not being so hard on myself when I do fail. I am after all changing some long time patterns of behavior and that doesn't happen overnight.**

Growing old with grace and style takes work. Growth always is a challenge and it takes effort. I know if I am going to live my old age even close to my dream and vision of the possibilities that I need to be working on it today. My hope and dream is if I practice being flexible and open to change now, I will be better able to manuiver through my own Aging Journey with **Pizzazz, Grace, and Style.** If I practice being interested in what is going on in my children's lives now, as their own experience and life moves them in their own unique direction; then when I am very old I can appreciate their experiences and keep reflecting back the special qualities I see in them. **It seems to me that it's much more pleasant to be around someone who reflects back your goodness and value rather than a person who is always complaining that you don't do enough or that you are not the person you expected them to be.**

## "I have lived to eighty-five, now the world owes me"

Have you ever heard someone say, "I'm eighty-five now and I shouldn't have to deal with all of these problems"?

"I 'should' be able to live in my home forever no matter how inconvenient it is to keep me there safely."

"My children owe it to me to disrupt their family, their work, their social life, to take care of me in the way I want to be cared for".

**Who ever said that in our 'Golden Years' we would be immune to the problems of the human race? Where is it written in any spiritual book that once past a certain age we will never again have to deal with problems related to our children, grandchildren, neighbors, government.** Where is it written that 'our' world should be centered on our needs irrivelent of the cost emotionally, physically, or financially just because we happen to be old? **A hard cold fact it that there is no age that makes us exempt from the normal problems that affect all human beings at one time or another.** Another hard cold fact is most likely someday we will have to leave our beloved home and be cared for by strangers. The family supports and neighborhood supports of the past no longer exist. **A hard cold fact is that if we don't make decisions surrounding these issues then someone will make the decision for us, and it may be an overworked health care professional who isn't really interested in the quality of our life.**

# Following our patterns of living

Often the end of our lives goes in the same direction and follows the same path that we created in our younger years. If we were critical demanding, and selfish when we were younger, we very likely will continue to be that way when we get old. **Our only hope is to began working at expanding our vision today.**

# We are always the creators of the quality of our lives

**It has never been someone else's responsibility to make us happy.** We are responsible for our own happiness and our own social life. It is not our childrens job to be our whole social network. It is not our children's job to provide meaning and purpose for our life. Just as it was not our job to provide these things for our own children. If we try to push these responsibilities off on our children we create chaos in their lives as well as our own. We set ourselves up for disappointment, anger, and bitterness.

I loved my children more than life itself, but I never expected them to meet my social needs. I never expected them to meet my financial needs. And when they were teenagers, I was grateful when they even liked me. I have no right to expect them now to be everything to me when they have husbands, jobs, and their own children.

I want to be grateful whenever my children choose to include me in the circle of their life. I have not been the center of my children's lives since they were babies. If I have such a need to be the center I need to go back in my memory bank and consider those wonderful moments when my children were babies and enjoy that memory for a while.

**After a time being warmed with these memories, it's time to do what I need to do in order to make my life work today**. I need to find more of the things that bring pleasure to my life on a daily basis. I need to make the effort to keep moving. And most of all I need to remember that

# happiness is a choice I make

**to focus on what is going right in my life rather than what isn't working quite the way I expected**

# Chapter 7

## Saying Goodbye

Saying goodbye to those we love is one of life's more painful tasks. We all must do it. We usually do it kicking and screaming at the unfairness of losing someone we care about deeply.

Death will come into each of our lives and we must find a way to go on living after losing those we depended on, and loved. Our lives were touched deeply by these persons, and we find it difficult to see how we will continue to live day to day without them.

*The author Melody Beattie wrote this in her meditation book, Journey of the Heart* about the death of her son.

"After losing my son, I found myself at a point where I simply could no longer stand the agony of waiting for my pain to disappear, I knew that all my life I would miss him, and I became absolutely despondent. I was waiting for this pain to disappear so I can begin living my life again. But the pain never will disappear."

Part of saying goodbye is recognizing that the pain will always be there in some form, but we can begin once again to live our lives with the pain walking right beside us. Sometimes something will trigger this pain of loss and it seems we are right back where we were when our loved one died. at those times we need to take time to

## be gentle with ourselves.

Take the time to write a letter to the person you are missing. Look at some pictures that remind you of happier times. Call a friend and talk about your feelings. These are some ways of

61

sitting with the pain until the intensity passes and we can go on with whatever we were doing when this feeling came over us.

**When we lose our parents** we lose our past. We lose a part of our identity, those people who impacted our lives from birth to adult hood are gone. These people were always there for us to bounce ideas off and to share humorous memories from the past. Many persons after losing their parents say they feel like they have been orphaned, and there is a sense of confusion that may last quite a while.

I have an image that has helped me with the deaths of my family generation before me. I felt a great loss after each death but when the last one died it made it final, that generation of my fathers family are all gone. One day in meditation I realized that each person I have loved is a permanent part of who I am. Little parts of them are deep inside my being. I am who I am because to the combined influence they have each had in my life. They are never really gone, because I have loved them and they live in me. I think of these people I have loved dancing in my heart, and this gives me a warm joyous feeling. At my own death, I envision that I will just move on to another level and be once again with these people who have never really left me.

**When our siblings die** we face our own mortality.

We recognize that we too will die. We lose those persons who were part of our childhood, and who helped in forming our identity. Often this brings up feelings of powerlessness, and guilt from the past. Sometimes we have left over business in our relationship with this person. We will need to decide if we want to resolve the issue if there is time, or let it go. We may not even have that option if someone dies suddenly. Everything doesn't fall into a neat little packages at our loved ones death. There are always things we wish we would have said or that we didn't say. We need to let these regrets go, as best we can. We have no power to change anything now.

**Death of friends** can also be devastating. These are the people

## we have chosen to walk beside us.

These are often our alter egos. Our friends love us warts, wrinkles and all. we have often shared deep moments that are difficult to share with family. **Our friends see our weaknesses, but choose not to focus on our flaws.** When friends die, we are left with a gaping hole where their love used to be. I remember getting a card after a lost love when I was younger. The card read,

## Sometimes when one person's gone the whole world seems empty

Like with other losses, we must learn to go on and continue living. I believe that our friends also become a part of who we are today. They to some extent live on inside of us as we live and hold dear the memory of friendship shared over our lifetime..

**If the death of a friend leaves a gaping hole, the death of a spouse is like having a body part removed.** Our spouse has seen the best and the worse in us for a long time, we often have lived with our spouse longer than we have with anyone else, even our family. Our spouse was our other half. They were constant in our lives. Hopefully our spouse was also our friend, but even those who had stressful relationships with their spouse, had a shared home, children, assets, and labor in the home. Often when a spouse dies we lose one income. We must learn to do the things that our spouse usually did around the home. We must identify ourselves in a different way. We are no longer a wife or husband. We now have an identity that is separate from anyone else. It becomes overwhelming for us to do this when the pain in our heart is so deep.

After a spouse dies the remaining spouse is at risk of serious illness especially, during the first year. We need to be gentle and patient with ourselves. We may need to talk about our loved one, and we need someone to listen to our pain. Sometimes, friends and family get tired of hearing about our loss day after day. This is when it may be helpful to go to a grief support group, a counselor or spiritual advisor who can listen and help us see hope of new beginnings. Our family are frequently going through their own grieving for a brother, sister or parent. **Death of an adult child** can be particularly painful to us. as parents we expect to die first. It feels unnatural for our children to go first. This is a loss of our dreams, and hopes for our adult child's life. We gave them birth, we put so much love and time into bringing them from infancy to adulthood. We may have expected them to help us in our old age and now they won't be here.

We must go on living our life in spite of the pain in our heart. We need to continue to

## find moments of joy

while holding those qualities we loved in our child close to our heart. We often need to work on forgiveness, of ourselves, the universe or the God we believe in for taking our adult child so soon.

Finally we come to face our own death. When it's time for us to move out of this life into the next, we must say goodbye. We say goodbye to our future and make peace with our past. We need to make peace with whatever higher power we believe in. We must clarify whatever it is we believe about an afterlife, a heaven, reincarnation, or going back into the earth. I think we also need to look at our past, and be peaceful about our failures and our successes. If we have done the work along the way of saying goodbye to the many losses we have encountered it may be less lonely and frightening to face our own death. There is no right way to take this final journey. It is our path and we should be able to make some of the decisions about how this occurs.

It is our journey and we must walk it alone.

Sometimes our family will try and hold on to us even when we are ready to go on. Hopefully, as we go through this phase of our lives we will have time to say goodbye to persons we love, to hold their hands and let them know we care. It is not just people we must say goodbye to. Last year I had to say goodbye to my hometown, as I knew it. I grew up in New Orleans, Louisiana. The hurricanes last year have made it unrecognizable. Places that have been part of my life forever are simply gone in the blink of an eye. I have cried many tears, I have been angry with the political systems who have not helped our people to rebuild, I have been angry at the people who are trying to destroy the city again with gangs and violence. But mostly I feel so very sad. I have spent this whole year saying goodbye to the city I knew.

Some people may rebuild, I believe that many will find a way to return to their roots and their culture. We don't choose where our roots will be. We are, however, loyal to those roots, the heritage of the place we grew up in and called home. I don't believe that it will ever be the New Orleans I knew. Many places won't be back, many people won't be back. New cultures may come and become a part of the fabric of that city. So grieving comes in many ways and we must walk that road largely alone.

I guess it is up to us to find meaning in our losses. It is up to us to say our good-byes and try to move on with our lives. We can try to

# find pockets of joy

and moments of peace as we continue on our own journey until it is time for our own final good-bye.

# *Chapter 8*

# ARE WE UP FOR THIS?

So are we ready for this last phase of our life our journey into aging? We have learned that

## aging is not for sissies.

It takes hard work and effort to age with grace and style. It takes a willingness to accept losses--physical, mental, work, and loved ones. It takes a willingness to accept and embrace change—changes in the roles I became accustomed to, roles I was comfortable in, change in income, reduced work schedule, and retirement. It takes learning to be comfortable with an unknown future and the knowledge that I am moving toward the end of my life at an accelerated pace.

## There are also opportunities that come with aging.

We have the opportunity to redefine who we are and become the person we want to be in this time and place.

While my health is good I have the option of making decisions based simply on what I want to do. I can take off on a weekend trip or a month-long trip to whereever I want to go without having the conflicts with a job or small children to consider.

I can renew a relationship with my spouse that includes more romance, and spontaneous lovemaking in the middle of the day, if that is what we want. I can take a course at a community college on painting, knitting, scrapbooking, or just take a course about a subject that has always interested me. I can do volunteer work on my own schedule. **I can read**

**all day and not worry about what anyone else wants or needs.** If I am widowed I can develop new relationships with persons of the opposite sex.

These can be romantic or just for companionship. **I can make these choices for myself.** Remember when we were in the middle of child rearing how we longed for this kind of freedom? Well now we have it or will soon have it so **we might as well make the best of the good times.**

# Consideration of the needs of others

I am not implying that we don't consider the needs of others. But while our health is good and we are able, we should go for whatever dreams we have left that are realistic and possible. Making time for family and being a part of adult children's lives can be very rewarding for both sides.

After I had children my mother and I seemed to have more to talk about. There is nothing like an adult child starting their own family that takes away much of the blame and anger we carried over from adolescence. **When we are the ones responsible for making decisions for the good of our own children, we develop much more respect for the parenting of our own parents.** This can be a wonderful time to build up relationships that may have been strained during those years when we made the best decisions we could at the time, but maybe missed something important that one child needed. We can take the time to consider our mis-steps and ask forgiveness of our adult children.

We can develop adult relationships with our adult children and recognize the gifts they bring to their own families. We can remember that our adult children are just that. They are grown and are capable of making their own decisions about how they will live their life. It is no longer our business to intrude on our adult childrens lives by giving advice. I have a friend whose favorite line is

## never pass up an opportunity to keep your mounth shut.

Showing consideration to others means not judging the parenting, housekeeping and other decisions that our grown children make. I can remember when I was pregnant with our first child I would promise this unborn child that I would never make the same mistakes my parents made with me. **And I didn't. I made new mistakes that were all my own, my children will have to**

**live with their impact on their lives maybe forever.** This is not something to beat ourselves up about. We all make mistakes. And our children will make their own mistakes which their children will have to live with. **We need to let our children who are now adults have the same privatlege and respect the choices they are making in terms of raising their own children.** We don't want to be the kind of person who walks into an adult child's home and notices the dirt almost before we are in the door.

If we have no children we can make time for friendships both, new and old. And don't let them slip away without a proper good bye. There may never be a friend like one you knew for forty or more years, but new friends are exciting too. **You get to tell all of your old stories and there is no one there to correct you if you inflate the details some.**

## Keeping our Circle Open

Let's not forget the importance of keeping our circle of life open. **It will shrink soon enough without any additional help from us. Make it a point to do something new at least once a month, and preferably once a week or even once a day.** That keeps our mental sharpness going longer. It challenges our mind and keeps us agile mentally and emotionally. **The longer we can keep moving and learning we can continue to improve the quality of our life each day.**

## Planning for Fun

What gives meaning to my life? What do I enjoy? In planning for fun in my life, I have to know what it is that gives me pleasure in my life. Often we spend much of our child-rearing years thinking about what is fun for our children. We may have time to learn about what we enjoy after they leave home and start their own lives, but we may also be working and just doing what we have to do each day without giving much thought to what we truly enjoy. **We think that on that magic day that we retire we will learn to have fun.** Most people have lots of "reasons" why they don't have fun and pleasure in their lives. **Often it is just a matter of just letting life go on as it always has, not thinking about what we are choosing on a daily basis.**

When we were younger we planned vacations carefully. We chose places we wanted to see, looked at what we had to spend on vacation, and tried to do as much as we could within the time and money we had. That was usually just a once a year event. Why not start now planning for things we enjoy, things we want to do but never had time for when we were younger? I believe it is very easy when we retire not to make plans, to just float through days and miss so many opportunities. I had my children late, so I am sixty-two and still have a teenager at home. Sometime in the past few years I decided that **I needed to find out what I enjoyed doing**.

**I needed to make plans to fit those things I enjoyed into my life now and not wait till later.** Some of the things I have discovered that I enjoyed that are not costly are music, writing poetry, working on my family tree, reading, gardening, making scrap books with all the photos we have taken over the years, walking, visiting with friends. I also enjoy traveling. Visiting out of town family. I want to take a cross country trip by car. That has to wait till I retire, but I can plan some short trips to places that I haven't been to before. I may have to do some of these trips alone. My husband is not one for driving long distances or taking a four hour trip for just a weekend. But that is ok it doesn't mean I can't do it.

One thing I need to improve on in my life is increasing my friendships. I have wonderful friends but not many live close now. In the process of raising children, working, and holding a marriage together, I let many friendships dwindle. It is now hard for me to reach out to new people. I don't feel as secure as I once did. It is defintely an area I need to work on. I enjoy learning new things. I want to take some courses at our community college just for fun. I decided this year to go back to graduate school, a daunting but exciting decision. Hospitals have a high rate of cocane babies, or babies that just need to be held. They need volunteers who just hold babies. I think that would be a wonderful way to give my time. I have always been interested in political action. When I was younger in the sixties and seventies I enjoyed getting involved in making a difference by speaking out for those who had no voice. As I have more time I can get involved again in this kind of activity.

# The point is to identify what you might enjoy and try it

**If it turns out that this activity doesn't speak to your soul then try something different.** If we don't have a plan we may just miss out on some very fullfilling and interesting times in our life.

# ACCEPTING OUR FAILURES

We do at some point in our life need to recognize that we didn't do all the things we wanted to do.

We didn't become the person we thought we were going to become. We made some poor choices along the way that made a difference in where we stand today. It's ok. We did the best we could with the information we had at the time. This is where we are today, financially, emotionally, and physically.

## It's never too late to maximize the time we have left.

Sitting around beating ourselves up is no benefit to anyone.

## Find something that builds you up and do it now

# Planning your Funeral

I have been planning my funeral since I was in my twenties. Because I worked in the medical field and had often become close to the people I worked with, I attended many funerals. I decided a long time ago the kind of music I wanted, the scripture readings I wanted, who I wanted to speak at my funeral. Unfortunately the person I really wanted to speak died some time ago, but I still have my plan it just needs to be revised a little.

I want my funeral to be

## a celebration of the life I have lived.

Yes, I know my family will miss me, but I want them to remember that life is a circle with a beginning and an end. **Anyone who has touched us will always be a part of who we are.**

**I know that I will be a part of the lives of the people I touched just as those I have loved will continue to be a part of who I am every day that I live.** I want my family to be able to celebrate the fact that we were a part of each other's life. I want them to carry with them some of the gifts I was privileged to share with them.

**I want to be sent off with the sound of jazz, bright colored baloons, a bright red dress, long ear rings, glitter in my hair, and a kiss in the wind as I join those people who were part of my circle who are waiting for me on the other side.**

Let us go through this journey together and share stories, and encourage each other as we move into old age.

**We still have something to say about how we are treated in this world. Let's not leave the planning for our future to health professionals, government bureaucrats, or anyone else.**

# Let's plan this one for ourselves

We have an opportunity to make a difference by the sheer numbers of us coming rapidly into old age.

**Let's do it with**

Kate Miller was born in New Orleans, Louisiana. She now lives in Overland Park, Kansas and has been working as a social worker in the Kansas City metropolitan area, for the past 26 years. Most of her work has been in the field of home health care, and her work with the elderly has spanned her whole career. Before going into social work she was a nurse. She is currently married and has two children. Her husband was recently diagnosed with Alzheimer's. She continues to work full time in home health. And currently has no plans to retire.

www.ingramcontent.com/pod-product-compliance
Lightning Source LLC
Chambersburg PA
CBHW080841250626

47161CB00009B/3149